MARVEL SUPER HEROES

World of Reading

LEVEL 1

THIS IS SPIDER-MAN

By **Thomas Macri**
Illustrated by **Todd Nauck** *and* **Hi-Fi Design**
Based on the Marvel comic book series **The Amazing Spider-Man**

MARVEL
New York

Published by Marvel Press, an imprint of Disney Book Group. No part of this book may be reproduced or transmitted in any form or by any means, electronic or mechanical, including photocopying, recording, or by any information storage and retrieval system, without written permission from the publisher. For information address Marvel Press, 114 5th Avenue, New York, New York 10011-5690.

This is Peter.

Peter lives in Queens.
Queens is in
New York City.

Peter lives with his aunt.
Her name is Aunt May.

Peter loves Aunt May
very much.

Peter is a student.
He goes to high school.

Peter loves school.
He loves math.

He loves science.

Some kids at school are
not nice to Peter.

They push him.
They make fun of him.

Peter does not care.

At home, no one makes fun
of Peter.

Peter has a super secret.

He has a costume.

He has web-shooters.

He makes webs.

He shoots webs.

This is his costume.
It has a spider on it.
It has webs on it, too.

Peter puts on his costume.
Peter has a secret name.

He calls himself
Spider-Man.

This is Spider-Man.

Spider-Man can climb
up walls.

He can swing on
his webs.

He shoots his webs.

His webs stop bad guys.

Peter takes off his mask.
He is tired.

Peter goes to sleep.

Peter wakes up. He gets
ready for school.

At school, the kids learn
about Spider-Man.

They like Spider-Man.

They do not like Peter.

But they do not know
Peter's secret.

Peter is Spider-Man.

World of Reading

LEVEL 1

THIS IS IRON MAN

By **Thomas Macri**

Illustrated by **Craig Rousseau** *and* **Hi-Fi Design**

Based on the Marvel comic book series **The Invincible Iron Man**

MARVEL

New York

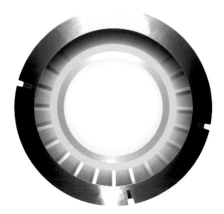

Published by Marvel Press, an imprint of Disney Book Group. No part of this book may be reproduced or transmitted in any form or by any means, electronic or mechanical, including photocopying, recording, or by any information storage and retrieval system, without written permission from the publisher. For information address Marvel Press, 114 5th Avenue, New York, New York 10011-5690.

This is Tony.

He owns a company.
It is called Stark.
Stark is also his
last name.

Tony is rich.

He has a beach house.

He has a house in
the city.

He has a boat that is big
as a house.
He has a house as big as
an island.

Tony has good friends.
He works with his friend
Pepper Potts.

Tony has a friend named
James Rhodes.
Tony calls him Rhodey.
Rhodey works for the army.

Tony has a secret.

Tony wears a disk.
It keeps him alive.

He made the disk.

But that is not all.

Tony has a bigger secret.
He keeps it in his case.

He keeps a suit with him.

He puts on the suit.

This is Tony's big secret.
He is a Super Hero!

Tony puts on his helmet.
He has a secret name.
He calls himself
Iron Man.

This is Iron Man.

Iron Man can fly.

He can shoot
repulsor blasts.

Iron Man shoots
his blasts.
They stop bad guys.

Tony's suit makes
him strong.

It makes him
a Super Hero.

Tony works to make his
suit better.

He tests new things.

He tries new suits.

The man inside is
the same.
He is Tony.

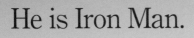

He is Iron Man.

World of Reading

LEVEL 1

THESE ARE THE AVENGERS

Adapted by **Thomas Macri**

Illustrated by **Mike Norton** and **Hi-Fi Design**

Based on the Marvel comic book series **The Mighty Avengers**

New York

Published by Marvel Press, an imprint of Disney Book Group. No part of this book may be reproduced or transmitted in any form or by any means, electronic or mechanical, including photocopying, recording, or by any information storage and retrieval system, without written permission from the publisher. For information address Marvel Press, 114 5th Avenue, New York, New York 10011-5690.

These are the Avengers.

The Avengers are a
team of Super Heroes.

Six Super Heroes are Avengers.

Each has a power.

Captain America is strong.

He has a shield.
His shield
cannot break.

He throws his shield
to stop bad guys.

It flies back.

Ant-Man is an Avenger, too.
He can become
as small as an ant.

Ant-Man can speak to bugs.
They help him win
his fights.

Ant-Man can also
make himself big.

Ant-Man calls himself
Giant-Man when he is big.

Ant-Man has a partner.
She is called Wasp.

Wasp is like Ant-Man.
She can become small.

She has wings.
She can fly.
She can sting.

This is the Hulk.
He is an Avenger, too.

The Hulk is big.
He is green.
He is very strong.

He can even smash bricks.

This is Thor.
Thor is also
an Avenger.

Thor has a hammer.
He uses it to fly.

Thor slams his hammer
to make thunder.

Thor throws his hammer.
It always comes back to him.

Iron Man is
an Avenger.

Iron Man is not a robot.
He is a man
in an iron suit.
His name is Tony.

Tony made the suit.

Tony is safer in the suit.
The suit is full of power.

Each hero is strong.

As a team they are stronger.

These are the Avengers.

World of Reading

LEVEL 2

THE STORY OF
SPIDER-MAN

Adapted by **Thomas Macri**
Illustrated by **The Storybook Art Group**
Based on the Marvel comic book series **The Amazing Spider-Man**

New York

marvelkids.com

TM & © 2012 Marvel & Subs.

Peter Parker didn't have
many friends.

Other kids thought Peter was
different. They made fun of him.
They liked sports and music.
Peter liked books.

Peter loved all his classes at school.
But he loved science the most.

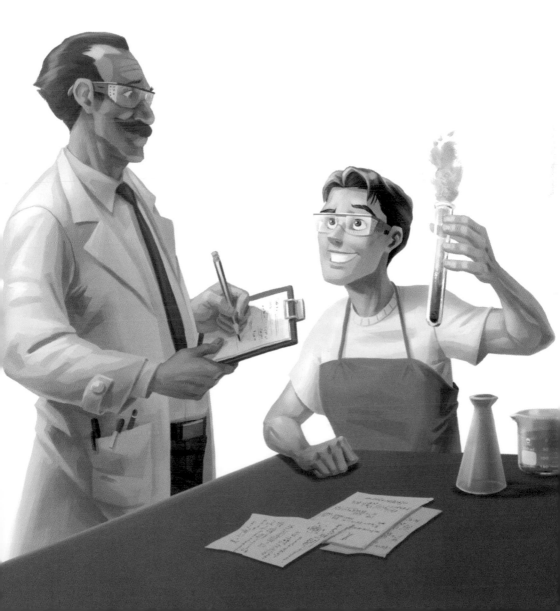

Peter only loved one thing more
than science. He loved his family.
He lived with his Aunt May and his
Uncle Ben. At home, Peter couldn't
have been happier.

Aunt May and Uncle Ben loved Peter. They bought him a new microscope. Uncle Ben told him that science was power. "And," he said, "with great power comes great responsibility."

One day, Peter heard that a lab was going to do something special. They were going to show how a ray worked. Peter visited the lab to see it.

The rays lit up. But a spider
dropped down between them.

The spider was zapped with power.

Peter didn't notice something.
The spider was falling down. And
it was falling on him!

The spider was glowing with power.
It bit Peter's hand.

Peter held his head. He felt sick.

Peter left the lab. He felt so sick that he almost didn't see a car coming.

He jumped out of the way.

He jumped higher than he thought
he could. He landed on a wall.
And he stuck to it!

He climbed up the wall. He was just like the spider that bit him!

He jumped from roof to roof. His
powers were like a spider's.
He must have gotten them from the
spider bite!

Peter was amazed by his powers.

Peter saw a poster of a wrestler.
He would test his powers on him.

Peter put on a mask. He challenged the wrestler.

He threw the wrestler.

He beat the wrestler!

Peter was happy. But he couldn't be a spider-man without something else. He went home and made some gluey stuff.

Then he made something to shoot the stuff. He called them web-shooters.

Peter made a costume. He called
himself Spider-Man!

People loved Spider-Man! They loved his powers. Soon he was famous.

But one night he saw a robbery taking place. A cop called out to stop the crook. But Peter didn't stop him. Peter was tired of being told what to do. So he let the crook go.

Peter went home. There were cops
outside. He knew something
was wrong. The cops told Peter
there had been a crime at his house.
Uncle Ben was the victim.

Peter put on his Spider-Man costume.

He rushed to find the criminal.

When he found him, Peter discovered
something terrible. The crook was
the same man he had let run away.

Peter was so sad he cried. But he remembered that Uncle Ben had told him with great power comes great responsibility.

He knew this meant he had to fight
crime. He would do it as Spider-Man.
He swung over the city.
A hero had been born.

THE STORY OF
IRON MAN

By Clarissa Wong
Illustrated by Craig Rousseau *and* Hi-Fi Design
Based on the Marvel comic book series The Invincible Iron Man

New York

marvelkids.com

TM & © 2012 Marvel & Subs.

Tony Stark was good at making stuff. He was so good that the army wanted Tony to help them.

Tony was working in a secret lab. There was an explosion! An enemy had attacked the lab!

They wanted to use Tony
to make weapons. They
took Tony away.

They took Tony to a prison cell.
There he met another prisoner.
His name was Yinsen.

Yinsen was a scientist. He put
a hand on Tony's shoulder.
He told Tony he was hurt.

Yinsen built something to help
Tony. It would keep Tony's
heart beating. He would
always have to wear it.
It would keep him alive.

They also built a suit of armor.
Tony would wear it. It would
make him strong. It would help
them escape.

In the suit, Tony could break through anything. He smashed through the brick walls.

He took on the whole enemy army!

He easily beat them.

The enemy was scared. They ran
away from Tony.

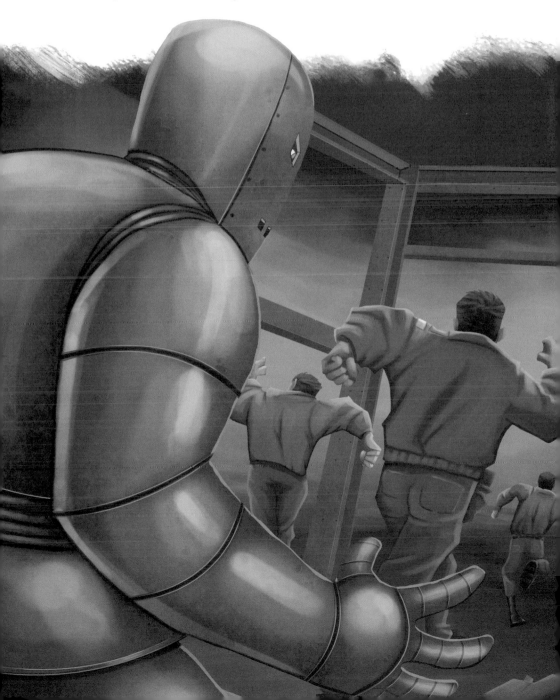

Tony was able to escape.
He used his suit to fly home.

Tony wanted to use the suit to
help others. On TV he saw there
was a crime happening.

Hc flew to the crime scene
to stop the crook.

But when he got there, people were afraid of him. His armor was too scary!

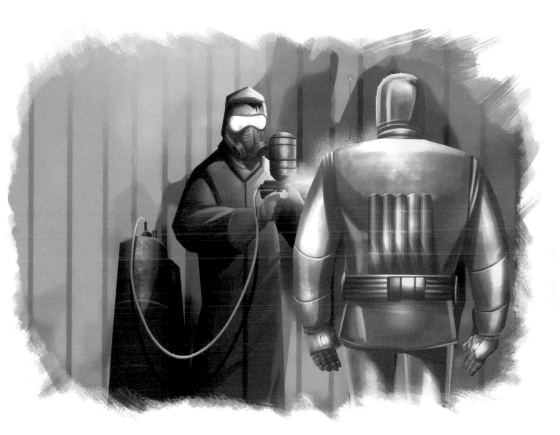

Tony painted his armor gold.
Now maybe people wouldn't
be scared of him.

But his armor was still not perfect
yet. He needed to fix it some more.

Tony kept working on his suit.
He made it lighter.

He painted it
red and gold.

He created a powerful
energy force.

Now he could shoot blasts
from his hands.

He could fire rockets from his boots. His suit could fly faster than ever before!

He had to think of a secret
Super Hero name for
himself.

He called himself
Iron Man!

Iron Man fought Super Villains.

Sometimes Iron Man had to fight
two Super Villains at the same time!

Iron Man could attack from behind.

He could even lift up a heavy
bad guy!

Tony always looked for new
ways to fix his armor.
He used special tools.
He put on his goggles
and worked all the time.

When he was not being
Iron Man, Tony was a
businessman. He ran
Stark Industries.

But Tony always kept a
suitcase nearby with his
Iron Man armor in it.

After all, he never knew
when the world would
need an Iron Man!

THE STORY OF
THE AVENGERS

Adapted by **Thomas Macri**
Illustrated by **Mike Norton, Pat Olliffe, Val Semeiks,** *and* **Hi-Fi Design**
Based on the Marvel comic book series **The Mighty Avengers**

New York

Super Villains did bad things.

But there was always a Super Hero
somewhere to stop them.
Thor fought giants in Asgard.

On Earth, Hulk smashed.
He had great power.

Far away, Iron Man
used his blasts.

Around the world, Ant-Man
and Wasp rushed into action.

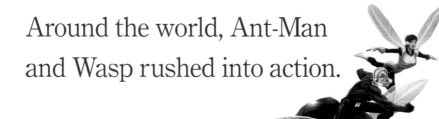

Wasp could become small.
She could shoot blasts.

Ant-Man could become small, too.
But he could also become big.
When he was big, he was Giant-Man!

One day a villain planned
something really bad.
The bad guy's name was Loki.

Loki's brother was Thor.

Thor was a Super Hero.

He had a great hammer.

It helped him beat bad guys.

Loki was jealous of Thor.
Loki used the Hulk to lure Thor.

Loki tricked people. He made them
think the Hulk had smashed train
tracks. He knew Thor would rush
to the rescue.

Ant-Man and Wasp flew over.

So did Iron Man.

They met at the train.
Loki's brother, Thor, was there, too.

Iron Man, Ant-Man, and Wasp
flew off to find the Hulk.

But Thor went to find Loki.
He knew he was the real villain.

The heroes attacked the Hulk.

They thought he was a bad guy.

But Thor brought Loki to them.
He held him up.
He told them Loki was the real
bad guy.

The Super Heroes fought Loki
and won!

They couldn't have done it alone.

They decided to form a team.

They called it the Avengers!

They fought together.

They beat bad guys who were too tough to fight alone.

One battle took the team
to a frozen land.

There, the Avengers
spotted a man in ice.
Giant-Man swam to the man.
He grabbed him and brought
him back.

Iron Man used his rays to melt
the ice.
He had to be careful.
He didn't want to burn the man.

The man in the ice was
Captain America!

He was a hero from long ago.
He had a mighty shield.

Captain America was confused.
He had been lost for a long time.
He didn't know these Super Heroes.

Iron Man put a hand on his shoulder.

Suddenly, the Avengers were attacked.
The bad guys were all around them.

Cap's shield flew by.

He helped the Avengers beat
the bad guys!

The team was finally complete.
Cap had joined them. Now, no one
could ever beat them.
The world could always count on
the Avengers!